art is fleeting

I0679197

art is fleeting

a collection of very short stories

rachel rodman

SHANTI ARTS PUBLISHING
BRUNSWICK, MAINE 04011

art is fleeting
a collection of very short stories

Published by Shanti Arts Publishing
Cover and interior design by Shanti Arts Designs
Cover and interior image by Marc Sendra Martorell
at unsplash.com

Shanti Arts LLC
193 Hillside Road
Brunswick, Maine 04011

shantiarts.com

ISBN: 978-1-956056-00-6 (softcover)
ISBN: 978-1-956056-01-3 (ebook)

Library of Congress Control Number: 2021945871

Contents

Acknowledgments

The author wishes to thank the editors of the following publications in which these pieces previously appeared:

Apparition Literary Magazine: "A Son"

The Cafe Irreal: "Grandchild," "In Enthusiastic Answer to a Question That No One Was Asking," " . . . Just Start Salivating," "Perhaps I Cannot Hold a Candle to You. But I Can Set You on Fire," and "When Nietzsche Met Quantum Physics Met Galileo"

City. River. Tree.: "Are You?" and "Pedigree"

Curiouser Magazine: "Our Song"

Daily Science Fiction: "Dorothy," "For the War Effort," "Six Nights, Six Monsters," and "The Quantum Womb"

Dreams and Nightmares: "The Greatest" and "The Velveteen Kitten"

Eastern Iowa Review: "Frosty: A Man for All Seasons"

Expanded Horizons: "Alternative Histories"

Fireside Fiction: "The Gingerbread Pox"

Frozen Wavelets: "Time Flies Even When You're Not Having Fun"

The Future Fire: "Seven Choices"

Grievous Angel: "Four Christmas Miracles"

Illumen: "Darkness" and "What It's All About"

The Journal of Compressed Creative Arts: "A (Condensed) Dictionary of Mythological Characters" and "The Withholding"

Mithila Review: "Different Boxes"

New Reader Magazine: "Everyone" and "Red Christmas"

Page & Spine: "I Luncheth with Mine Enemies" and "We Seem to be on the Same Wavelength about the Fact That Each of Us Is Operating on an Entirely Different Wavelength"

Sein und Werden: "The Agnostic Gospels: Variations on a Theme"

The Ultra-Short: Fourteenth Annual Competition (published by The Primavera Press): "A Dream of Rome"

The Weird and Whatnot: "In My Calendar" and "Russian Doll"

Zetetic: A Record of Unusual Inquiry: "Dorothy II"

We Seem to Be on the Same Wavelength about the Fact That Each of Us Is Operating on an Entirely Different Wavelength

"Roger that," I said into the microphone crisply.

But then it all dissolved into static.

My Saber Is Not Made of Light

"Are you still conflicted?" asked my master. "Do the dark and the light continue to war within you?"

I closed my eyes. "No," I said finally.

"Then—?"

"I have chosen the gray side of the force."

"But—" said my master.

"Nice tunic," I said, not really meaning it.

A Dream of Rome

It was the fashion in those times, recalling the grandeur of Rome and the non-conventional childhood of Romulus, its founder, for parents to entrust their offspring to wolves.

As swaddling cloth, the parents used silken fabrics, monogrammed with the family crest. With particular care, they wrapped the little hands that would one day build iconic civilizations.

In hollows by the river, the parents set their bundles. Before leaving, they waited for the telltale glitter of teeth set in the underbrush, evidence of a she-wolf waiting to complete the adoption.

"Be great," they instructed their babies by way of goodbye.

She Swallowed the Pipers
to Catch the Lords . . .

. . . And I don't know *why* she swallowed the partridge in a pear tree. Perhaps she'll die.

Dorothy

It was a chaste courtship. Her lust was constrained by her conservative upbringing; his, by his lack of a central nervous system.

Often, they simply talked. She chatted extensively about her life in the old world before the tornado. She had loved, she said, her school and her church, and the little farm with the painted weathervane, and the baby chicks, haloed in adorable fluff.

He never actually said anything. Occasionally, a breeze would catch the back of his head, and he gave what appeared to be a nod. On his face, stitched in thread, there was a permanent smile. To a part of her—which was very lonely—these were thrilling things.

She remained with him for several days, delaying her journey. She slept below and apart, close to the yellow bricks, while he remained on his pole.

On the third day, she had a strange thought.

On her neck was a chain, a gift at her baptism. From it dangled a man—a miniature, made of pewter. Now she removed it.

Holding it up, she compared them. Old and new. The first, an iconic figure whom she had always reverenced.

The second, a new friend. Just a pleasant man made of cloth who brought her so much comfort.

And yet . . . they were the same. Their limbs were constrained at the same pathetic angles, each forcibly affixed to a framework of wood.

In the shock of it, the pewter man slipped from her fingers, and she looked only at the cloth one.

She experienced a jumble of feelings. Guilt, shyness. Concern for his suffering. But a warmer emotion most of all.

The first nail, at the bottom, snapped easily. To reach the other two, she had to climb the post.

The witch's shoes were clunky, and this made the going hard. Below, too, Toto was barking. A warning, maybe. Or jealousy.

In the middle, she found a secure position. From it, she was able to reach over both sides. After a little work, each hand dropped free. Left, right. Straw trailed from the holes.

He weighed almost nothing. It was so easy to support him.

"Marry me," she said quickly while she still had breath enough, before her nerve deserted her. Flickers of memory, of playing "nuns" as a child—the conceit of it, which she had never fully outgrown, of serving as a bride of Christ.

"Yes," he said as a gust penetrated his porous head and jostled the straw adjacent to his mouth. "Yes . . . yes . . . yes . . ."

Very, Very Drunk on Very Little Power

"There's a form to fill out," I informed her from behind my desk—giddily, slurringly, and with a little hiccup.

"Will you get it for me?" she asked.

"Maybe," I said.

Chekhov's Unicorn

He retained the thumb-sized animal on a ledge above his fireplace, set within a marble field, which was delimited on two sides by stacks of his completed plays. And here, on a thin layer of pixie dust, the animal grazed, quietly majestic, its tail flicking, its horn and mane shimmering—silver and white.

But that's not what this story is about.

A Son

He was the wrong kind of prince—a frog prince, a prince from the sort of fairy tale no girl had ever wanted.

And just when she began to suspect, a little, from the cadence of his blinks—and many other small things— that something was not right, he disappeared, with a lumbering hop, out into the marshlands, never to return.

The frog baby—his baby—was green and neckless and had webbed toes. It rejected her breasts; it did not want her milk.

"Ontogeny recapitulates phylogeny," the baby ribbited solemnly, defensively, after she gave birth to it.

It was born young, after just four months. And with its little speech, it seemed to assert that its awful abnormality was the result of its prematurity and not something more inherent, as if it was born just a bit before that point where most babies cease to be frogs. Otherwise, see, it would have been perfectly normal.

As if—goddammit—there were such a point.

"What a little twerp," she thought. "What a shameless liar."

But instead she said, "Oh." And with an effort, grinding her teeth, she converted the flame-hot flare of her anger into sadness.

Princes deserve respect, after all. And she was only a peasant. So she tucked her swollen breasts away and fed it flies and filth, for years, until metamorphosis set in, and it became, in fact, more-or-less a boy, with cold lips and slow eyes, precisely like its father's.

Back and Forth

"I'm going to abduct your children," she said—a gleam.
"I'm going to brutalize them. And then I'm going to
 devour them."

"Don't," I said.

"Ha ha," she said. "That was a joke." But her eyes still
gleamed. And her lips were open—wet.

"Oh," I said. And forced a smile.

For it was good to have friends.

What Happens When

"The only way *out* of Paradox," said the Unstoppable
Force, as It advanced, implacable.

"Is more Paradox," countered the Immovable Object.

So then time st—

Rome Took Me All Morning

"You know," she said at lunch, "what they say about cathedrals?"

I smiled. And cracked my knuckles.

"They take *centuries* to erect!" I said.

Then, with a manic laugh, and as she eyed me bemusedly, I gave my builder's kit—trusty and dusty— an affectionate kick.

My afternoon was free.

The Withholding

At her chest, in a drawstring pouch, she kept a personal hoard of rats' asses. They were worn and polished, like leather coins, with empty circles at their centers.

There she held them perpetually, warmed by her heart, so that whenever the right occasion arose, she could conspicuously *not* give them out.

"No," she would say, lips twisting and eyes slitted in a withering contempt. "This particular set of circumstances does not warrant anything that I have stored here."

Everyone

"How can *everyone* be faking it?" I protested. "Everyone else cannot possibly feel like this—like I do—all the time."

Her eyes crinkled in a way that, at first, I could not read. But then she blinked and I apprehended it—the misery, the *coldness*—so that, even at this faint intimation, lidded and brief, I wondered if I would ever again be warm.

"Fake harder," she advised me.

Would You Like Me to Rank Your Friends According to How Much I'd Like to Have Sex with Them?

Long pause.

Pregnant pause.

Long, long, long, long pause.

"No?" he said.

Scorpio to Scorpio

It was the fact, I think—it was almost certainly the fact—that I murdered seventy-three people, slowly and secretly, over an equal number of Sunday afternoons, after services, and then buried them in shallow graves beside the church that gave me away.

She, too, had her own bag. Her own shovel.

And we know our own.

"I can guess your sign," she said softly.

Second Verse, Same as the First

I wanted to bleed.

From the adjoining room, the sounds came: my nine-year-old, five-year-old, and three-year-old, shrieking and pummeling one another, feral amid filth.

And, as my urine ascended the testing strip, slow, slow, slow (and in my stomach, equally, the dread) I wondered: Did He remember me?

"Are you there, God?" I whispered, "It's me, Margaret."

We Argued in Italian

Your grandmother was Sicilian.

Mine was from Naples.

And when we fought, only those one-quarters mattered.

"Mamma mia!" you shouted.

"Figaro! Figaro!" I said, just so passionately.

"Spaghetti! " you spat, "Vermicelli!" And with each syllable, you flung the corresponding pasta against the wall—gooey and starchy.

"Fusilli!" I returned with parallel flings. "Penne! Orecchiette!"

This was the sum of our Italian vocabulary.

But language is about more than words.

In your bed, tucked beneath the covers, having devoted all morning to its procurement and murder, I placed a dead horse. A stallion.

You, on the other side of the covers, with similar deviousness, similar wrath, positioned another dead horse. A mare.

"Vendetta!" you screamed amid the hooves and hair while gesticulating with a gore-soaked pillow.

"Vendetta!" I said, leaping angrily onto the mattress springs, which squealed and groaned, already compressed by the corpses.

"Brutus!" you shouted—for Italian rage goes deep—and into the air you heaved a two-seater gondola, which, when I ducked, splintered violently against the headboard.

"Mussolini!" I mocked in return. And I followed up with the oars, for you had forgotten those.

Hadn't you?

Wet smash: pizza! Wet smash: pizza! Crust and cheese and tomato sauce, pepperoni on your face, mushrooms on mine. And I, in my fury, tore up all the notebooks of da Vinci, shredding them so small that whether they had been written forwards or backwards was no longer discernible. And you, from the wall, threw down his complete paintings—the *Mona Lisa* too—and ripped and ripped and ripped, so that the Lisa's inscrutable smile became still more inscrutable.

Obliterate! Annihilate! Tear, tear, tear!

And when we had only bits, we cast them into the air, earnestly and hatefully, toward one another's eyes— potent particulates, like the ash from Vesuvius, tiny and white.

Die, die, die!

Die.

Until, sinking back—nothing left to rip, nothing left to throw—against the bloated, stinking horses, the ruined mattress, and distended springs; the pasta falling around us, detaching sporadically from the walls as it dried, soft and slow.

We looked at one another.

And we would remember something else.

That we had other grandparents.

Yours was a smoking Parisian intellectual, *une machine pour* converting cigarette smoke into nihilistic philosophy.

Mine was from the vineyards, adjacent to Dijon, pacing and stomping amid the rows of familial grapes, the soles of his feet stained congenitally purple.

Blood memories of fresh baguettes, conveyed miles and miles beneath damp armpits. Berets and conjugal positions, poetry and escargot. Vowels inflected, sexual R's.

Circumflexes. Language caressed.

All in tongues.

So we made up in French.

Poop-cocious

Another birthday.

Amid the party preparations, she appeared to us—
again—in the doorway, with a familiar shuffling gait.

And a guilty smile.

"She's *four*," I whispered to him after it was over, the
clean-up.

"Not precocious," he averred.

If I Am This Emotionally Transgressive When I Am Being Nice to You, Just Imagine What an Enemy I Would Make!

"Friends forever," I agreed, swallowing hard.

Darkness

Once it was cut away, it dove down, as far and as deep as it could possibly go—irretrievable, perhaps, but not exactly lost.

Because, now, whenever you look in that place where you never grew up—where you couldn't, Never-Never, where you *couldn't*, NEVER-NEVER—everything is still there, still raw, and inescapable, and it is as if the intervening years have not happened at all.

Because now, whenever you stare into the Abyss, there is Peter Pan's shadow, staring back at you.

Brainstem Storming

Inhale.

Heartbeat.

Exhale.

Food?

Sex?

Sex with Food?

Inhale.

Heartbeat.

Exhale.

And Baby Makes One

"You're not my mother," she said accusingly after she had tracked me—us—down through the obfuscatory layers of paperwork.

And through time.

"Not my mother," she repeated with a note of growing wonder. "You're me."

"Yes. And . . . ," I said, both affirming and correcting. (And struggling, a little, for breath.)

Then, in a moment, with a small grunt, I gave birth, squatting within my skirts, to her, to me—to both of us, all of us—together and alone, in the midnight stillness of the maternity ward.

I caught the sticky infant, securely and two-handed, and she cried for only a moment before I brought her to my breast.

I had—in a sense—done this before.

And *she*, the other me, watched us, still a little stunned, still a little wary, and I could sense this in the periphery, even through my exhaustion.

But even more, I remembered it.

"Can I hold . . . me?" she asked finally, once the infant had fed. And her voice was soft.

No more accusations.

"Us," I corrected her. (Me.) And then I handed her (us) over, across a short distance, and at a constrained angle, for the umbilicus was still intact.

To myself.

"Family," I said, with a second whispery grunt, the placenta. Further explanations would wait.

We were both patient.

And I—she—nodded, looking down at me.

(At us.)

Then up again, back, to me—one look, simultaneous, but also across decades, mirrored.

And our eyes filled with tears.

Chivalry Is Dead

Ever since Its death—dating precisely, in fact, to
the moment of it—we had been feeling spiteful and
ungenerous.

Churlish.

"I don't think It *deserves* a burial," I said, curling my lips
contemptuously above Its helmed head.

So we left It to rot.

Unconditionally

In her eyes, I saw myself: not reflected.

But rather: bizarrely distorted.

"You understand *absolutely nothing* about me," I said.
And some of it—yes—was anger. But most of it was
wonder. "Not a single word I've ever—"

"ZZXFLGJ?" she returned lovingly. "XJCJV TYW?"

But the Third Brother
Was Very Spiritual

"I know!" cried Jasper. "I know how we can fly! Let's mash together a . . . a . . . paste from bits of birds, insects, and bats! And pterodactyl bones! And the spirits of these deceased beasts, once rubbed into our skins, will create a powerful aura that will enable us to levitate!"

His smile was rapturous; his eyes were beseeching and bright.

"*Then*, brothers!" he said, and as he spread out his arms, angel-like, he mimed the action of stepping into empty air. "Then we will soar!"

"Hmm," said Wilbur.

"No," said Orville.

It Wasn't a Threat, She Often Said; It Was a Promise

"Don't," I whispered.

But there was no going back on a promise.

PTSD

Maybe, this time, it will work out differently

It is imperative, after all, that it should

So you relive/remember/rehearse it, relive/remember/
rehearse it, relive/remember/rehearse it, relive/
remember/rehearse it, relive/remember/rehearse it

Until you are only the event, all the extraneous parts
worn away, and there is nothing else

Maybe, this time, it will work out differently

It is imperative, after all, that it should

So you relive/remember/rehearse it, relive/remember/
rehearse it, relive/remember/rehearse it, relive/
remember/rehearse it, relive/remember/rehearse it

Until you are only the event, all the extraneous parts
worn away, and there is nothing else

Nothing.

How Many Units of Tree-Derived Cellulose Would the Burrow-Dwelling Mammal, *Marmota monax*, Be Able to Extract and Process into Saleable Bundles, If the Burrow-Dwelling Mammal, *Marmota monax*, Could Extract and Process Tree-Derived Cellulose into Saleable Bundles?

"Catchy," sneered my editor, uncapping her pen.

Old Story

Her prince arrived, gallant on horseback.

But she chose Sneezy.

... Just Start Salivating

Across countries, across time, they began their duet—
Donne with his parchment, Pavlov with his dogs.

A hybrid verse, and they chimed it together, one voice,
one song: "Do not ask for whom the bell tolls ... Do not
ask ... "

We listened, beautiful—ding, ding, ding—absolute in
our focus.

We listened open-mouthed.

The Quantum Womb

The box was composed of flesh—living, human, maternal.

And, inside the box, a scattering of molecular confetti, sourced from two parents, swirled and shimmered, collided and collaborated, in an innumerable array of unprecedented arrangements—every way and no way.

To create . . . a birl.

And it was a president and a CEO with more power than a god; and a beggar, starving in a dumpster; and a soldier, bleeding in a ditch; and a professor of mathematics; and a philanthropist; and an impressionist painter; and a sociopath; and a hospice nurse; and a bureaucrat chained to an anonymous desk. And an Olympian; and a sexual criminal; and a celebrity, famous for fame; and a murderer; and a scientist, weighted with Nobel Prizes; and a voice—The Voice—the voice of a generation; and a social pariah, eternally lonely. (And a thing and a thing and another and another, for which— yet—there existed no words.)

But then, on the screen, the box was opened, and these simultaneities condensed and narrowed and became unalterably discrete—the map of something singular.

"It's dead, actually," observed the sonographer gently.

Invitations

It got through, finally, like a little dart. This clubhouse, of years' duration, and I never knew of it.

"We only induct new people every six months," the president offered. "And we just voted . . . "

All of them awkward. All looking away.

"I have a club too!" I said, trying to breathe, while my fingers pressed the top sheet of a stack of wrinkled fliers. "Anyone can come. Everyone! Would . . . ?"

"No," they said.

You Are Mentally Ill; and
You Know a Bit of Latin

"But you aren't magical," he finished.

"Really?" I dared him.

Constrained by my strait jacket, I could not quite reach my wand. So, as he continued to stare at me sadly, I flared my nostrils instead.

"*E pluribus unum*," I said darkly.

Intimate

She looked up, startled, from the open, broken thing, when I opened the door.

My . . . diary.

A moment, then—a beat—before my anger even began, when my heart was simply broken.

"Violation," I whispered.

"Hmm," she said, correctingly, reprovingly. And as she stroked the pages, gentle and slow, her expression became languorous. "I like to think of this instead as an intimate relationship I have with you that you know nothing about."

At Her Father's Deathbed

Tattoos and belly button rings. Drugs and badly groomed boyfriends.

Art school. And poverty.

"I did everything I could to disappoint you," she spat at him, hissing through her tears.

"But you failed," he replied with a contrarian smile, something like a mirror.

Thirty Seconds

I had only half a minute with my hero, Sylvia Plath. That is how time travel worked. It would be my sole allotment.

Just a flash.

I was very, very nervous.

I stood there, heart pounding, in the kitchen of her London flat, with her little girl and newborn son, and her, of course. Plath, the only person whose work ever moved me; the only poet, in my estimation, there ever ever was.

Her.

No brain anymore. Just nerves. And . . .

"Hey, Sylvia," I blurted, inclining my head goofily, giddily, and with unmistakable emphasis toward the oven, "What's for dinner?"

In Enthusiastic Answer to a Question That No One Was Asking

When *I* was in Japan . . .

A picture of my genitals? Yes, I can send you a picture of my genitals!

In my first book . . .

Pass It On

Things went wrong, as they sometimes do, and I knew I would die.

In my arms, a newborn daughter. In my head, a blur of thoughts: grandchildren, great-grandchildren; and into that future, an urgent message to convey.

Hemorrhaging.

And there was no time.

So I set her tiny ear against my lips.

Job Opening

"Would you like to be friends?" she asked. There were scraps of meat on her lips, evidence of a feast of some sort—lusty and juicy, perhaps, at one point, if the blood were any evidence. But now only bones.

The remains of . . .

. . . my predecessor.

"Yes," I whispered, misty-eyed, emotional, and—even if my voice shook a little—deeply touched by this invitation, this opportunity, this prospect, this vision of . . .

Of.

Nevertheless.

Everything Else

The sex was bad. As was the holding hands afterward. And the rapport at mealtimes. And the conversation— all of it.

But . . .

I'm Really, Really Awkward

With a bored look—and a supremely confident one—
the monster faced me down.

"How do you propose to defeat me?" he asked with a
careless growl.

"I have a superpower," I said.

"A *superpower?*" he said.

"Yes," I said with a smile, bouncing on my toes, and I saw
him beginning to sense it: the wrong amount of space
I had created between us, simultaneously too little and
too much.

How did I manage that?

I saw him swallow—the first intimations. I saw his eyes
dart past my shoulder, then back; sweat in a trickle
down his neck.

"A superpower?" he said more faintly.

"Yes," I said, continuing to smile, continuing to bounce.

And I waited for him to guess.

Wavelength

"That was amazing," she said. "Let's do that again right away!"

"...couldn't possibly imagine," he said, "doing that again for at least another twenty-four hours!"

A pause. One beat.

"Jinx!" they cried.

Social Lubrication

Hihowareyou, he slurred. How-was-your-weekend, I returned all in an ooze. And then we slipped past one another with disorienting quickness—stumbly and lurchy; sticky and slick.

But it was better than actually touching.

The Igneous Demon-God Lizard Children Play House

One of her red eyes went up, scythe-shaped and mischievous. *Just imagine.*

And while the river flowed around us, and above and below us, viscous and ubiquitous, she presented to us, with a theatrical flourish, the props she had assembled— jagged simulacra of . . .

"Tea cups!" shouted Yarrbladh, and his tail thrashed madly.

"Wallpaper!" said Cuthblort, and her three hearts pulsed purple, shedding protons as they beat—radioactive.

"Tablecloth!" said Norgloth, expelling bubbles from his lowest row of nostrils. "Ceiling!"

"Placemats!" I said, and I experienced a shiver of pleasant anticipation, so intense that I almost felt cold, even as the rocks around us were burning.

"Yes, yes!" agreed Quognoereth. Her tone, though impatient, was touched with another quality too, one that commanded our attention and meant that she would always be the one who decided what we would play.

Charisma.

"And *now*," she said eagerly, magma swirling as she exhaled, and as she conjured for us, flash and boom, the remaining boundary of this shared—yet conceptually infinite—domestic space. "Let's pretend the lava is a floor!"

Time Flies Even When You're Not Having Fun

"This sucks," she observed from her infant crib/dorm room bunk/Peace and Marine Corps hammocks/C-section pre- and post-op surgery cot/Alzheimers' ward nursing home bed.

And it did.

Wine

We met for lunch. And as we waited for our Chardonnay, $15 a glass, the door to the kitchen flapped open, and we watched the waitstaff pouring out our order.

From a box.

"Straight from France!" I cried bitterly.

"Imported by medieval sommeliers!" Tara added.

And we chortled like mad people.

"We're drunk," I explained to a cluster of other patrons seated close to the bar who turned to look.

"Sloshed," said Tara, even louder.

But we weren't.

Pedigree

When I gave birth to puppies—part English bulldog, part Irish setter, with a one-sixteenth trace, too, of German shepherd, and possibly of dachshund—my husband, no student of genealogy, gave me a look.

Such a look.

And I was like, "Didn't you know?"

I Just Had a Passing Thought about Thumb Tacks and Felt Certain That the Other 800 People on This Mailing List Would Appreciate Hearing about It Too

Click!

Our Song

I met him during a performance of Cage's *4'33"*.

"Brilliant," we said, eyes meeting over our programs. Later, in the lobby, our hands brushed. The next weekend, over wine, over breakfast in bed, we smiled about it. And on the day we moved in together, a copy of the album was my present to him, but also—independently and simultaneously, surprise, surprise—his present to me.

Brilliant.

One night, many years later, after our children had left home, I explained the joke of it to a dinner guest.

"We 'listen' to it often," I said as she thumbed through our collection, then, at my nod, withdrew one of the albums. "It's silence!" I said, laughing. And to illustrate, I set it on to play. "For four and a half minutes."

Then I turned to look back at him—my husband—who was in the kitchen, starting the dishes. And my eyes were brimming. Twenty-five years. "No sound—"

But the words caught in my throat.

For he was staring back at me with a stricken expression—notes of betrayal and revulsion.

As if I were no one that he knew.

"You can't hear that?" he asked.

In the Throes

Other people were better than I was.

"It's okay," she said, attempting to comfort me. "Envy is a very powerful emotion."

I lifted my head out of the dismal pile of the sheets.

"There are other emotions?" I asked wonderingly.

Six Nights, Six Monsters

1

"Brains!" he began, a low moan. "Brains!"

"My name is Brianna," I corrected him.

2

We met in the glade, beneath the moonlight.

Eyes, bright. Tongue, wet.

"Sit," I said firmly.

3

"May I?" I asked of his wrappings.

"I'm *sleeping*," he said.

And I felt the sting of it, his rejection.

Like a curse.

4

From bar to bar I had gone, checking my scabbard surreptitiously.

Nothing.

Until . . .

In a dive on 17th, I saw it: the shining. And when I drew it forth, slightly, by the hilt, I saw that my ancient blade, Sting, had begun to glow.

"Hello," I said—a slow whirl.

Well, *hello.*

5

"Limbs!" I decided, "I *like* limbs."

"Oh, good," he burbled. And then slowly, shiveringly, he commenced to remove my scuba gear.

6

"I wish we could be together always," I said after he spent the night.

"Well," he said, tipping back my head so that my neck extended. "There *is* a way."

"I know," I said, eyeing the jars of dust on my dresser. "Open the shutters," I said softly to my bedside Alexa.

And I let in the sun.

I Luncheth with Mine Enemies

I squinted at it on the menu: *Forgiveness*, a clump of unappealing syllables, flanked by soft, suspicious consonants—Fff; Sss.

Like Welsh.

So I ordered gazpacho.

Cold.

"*Well*," I said brightly once the waiter had gone, and I smoothed my napkin carefully across my knees, over and over and then again, as if considering, as if there was some decision to be made: what we would talk about.

Pleasantries

"I'm persisting," I told her curtly, a short, sharp immersion in the inexplicable tragedy that was my life.

"Oh," she said, recoiling.

"And how are you?" I asked.

Retro

It was a sisterhood—almost a club—but of the most awful imaginable sort.

We all had dead children.

Dead little children. And the tragedy, that haze of absolutely irremediable awfulness, coating everything—it was like living in the nineteenth century.

Not here, not now, when children are not supposed to die.

So how were we coping? With a nineteenth-century kind of loss?

Fire with fire.

"Laudanum," I said with a smile.

"Opium," added Meghan, just so sleepily.

"Mercury," sighed Debbie, a tinge to her eyes, yellow and silver.

Mercury had been a medicine once.

"Cocaine," said Allyson, licking her lips.

"I've found God," said Gemma, doubling down, apparently—and hadn't she always?—a bit harder than the rest of us. "And the story of Heaven."

"Gemma," I said. For the others had frozen. And as I shook myself from my laudanum stupor, this nineteenth-century haze, I rushed to enfold her. For Gemma was my Gemma, more than the others'. We had met years ago—before—in the children's ward, amid a cloying ambiance of disinfectant and Salvation Army teddy bears.

And hope.

Gemma, Gemma.

Godammit, Gemma.

"This isn't a game," I said.

Don't You Just Feel—I Mean, How Could You *Avoid* Feeling?—That the Vast Amount We Have in Common Really Underscores the Fact That We Have Nothing in Common?

"I mean, not really," she said, in what may or may not have been genuine bewilderment (for there it was, exactly the difficulty), her eyes to my eyes, a funhouse mirror.

Tantric Urination

"Still peeing," I announced through the door, long after it might (to some) seem plausible—or possible—to be.

But I was.

Dorothy II

Her mother was a refugee, displaced by a tornado. Her father was a scarecrow, attached to a post.

They are both dead now. Mother died from a respiratory illness, brought on by some subtle difference between the atmosphere of Oz and that of her native Kansas. Father died during a damp season when a mold propagated through his insides, something like a cancer.

So it's just her left to represent them. A mixture of both.

Her skin is mottled, part flesh and part straw. Her bones are brittle. Her eyes, too, are weak, freckled with paint chips.

Inside her head, it's much the same. Beneath her soft skull, gray matter is entangled with yellow, which makes it difficult for the neurons to fire.

Down the brick road, she goes on crutches, each step a labor. As she hobbles, she imagines what it would be like meeting the wizard. She plots out her petition in what detail she can—as much, that is, as her severe cognitive handicaps permit her to.

"Fix me," she would say.

Red Christmas

She had wanted, six years before—just six years—her two front teeth.

And now this.

(Hadn't she wanted this?)

And to have it, really—and *so much*—so that it had bled, that morning, through her reindeer pajamas and into the sheets.

"Thanks," she said dutifully, directing her whisper to the near-empty cookie plate on the mantelpiece, just crumbs.

But it was oddly like weeping.

At First Sight

I scanned his face briefly, automatically, and almost unconsciously, as I did every face, intent upon a snap categorization: Attractive or unattractive—a fact to file before I disengaged.

(Pretend—you liar—that you don't do the same.)

But I couldn't decide with him.

I couldn't decide.

And after fifty years of intimate cohabitation, eleven cities and three children, six thousand sexual consummations and thirteen thousand bottles of wine, I simply couldn't decide.

So I kept staring.

Russian Doll

His first wife, Natasha, possessed a third arm. It emerged from the top of her skull. For much of their marriage, she kept it carefully hidden, bent beneath her hair.

As the years wore on—and her beauty wore away— her perpetual up-do thinned. Eventually, he spied her secret.

The deformity was unexpectedly extensive. Natasha did not survive the surgery.

By following the arm, however, and excavating through bone, he discovered a new woman. "Tasha" was young and lovely. Beneath her hair, too, before she hurriedly brushed it up, he spotted the flicker of extraneous fingers.

"Perfect," he said leeringly.

Bluffing, Not Bluffing

"Fives are trump," I say. And then I throw one down—a diamond—and splay the remaining cards beneath my chin like a disguise.

"What? No!" you begin, but I can read you—the flicker of the vein on your forehead; your breathing, rapid and shallow. The self doubt. "They're *not*..."

"Aren't they?" I say.

And I raise you an eyebrow.

Your play, friend.

The Transcendent Four

The Gospel of Ringo

He was born in a yellow submarine.

The Gospel of Paul

He was the egg man. He was the walrus. And He said,
"All you need is love."

The Gospel of George

In the temple, before the Pharisees, He went: "Goo
goo g' joob/Goo goo g' joob." And when they tortured
and brutalized Him, and then He hung there dying, He
repeated it: "Goo goo g' joob/Goo goo g' joob."

The Gospel of John

Until at last He ascended, like Lucy in the Sky, into
Strawberry Fields, forever.

All the Way Down

This new planet—and this became increasingly obvious to us the longer we explored—was composed of penises.

Entirely of penises.

Forests—soaring penises.

Animal life—an array of smaller penises, flapping floppily through the air or confined to the ground.

"It's penises," I announced to others from my perch at the microscope, mid-squint.

"Penises," said our chemist, and proceeded to lay out a new model—a molecular confusion of shafts and heads.

"Penises," confirmed our geologist.

"No electrons," said our subatomic physicist in a stupefied whisper. "No *quarks*. Just—"

Dithering at the Banks of the Rubicon

"I'm gonna, I'm a-gonna," I said vaguely as I swished my toes in the water.

But I wasn't.

Poof!

I presented her—a bundle.

He stared at her wonderingly—startling in miniature, wrinkled and warm, a single minute fist emerging from the cloth.

"*How?*" he whispered.

My insides ached. My outsides were mottled with permanent scars. And I was still bleeding.

"*How?*" he repeated—fear and awe.

I bowed—a flourish.

But a magician never reveals her secrets.

The Self-Appointed Guardian
of My Mental Health

"Sometimes . . . " I said meekly. ("Usually . . . " I suggested sotto voce.) (("*Whenever* . . . " I breathed—an echo of a whisper.))

" . . . in trying to help me, you actually make everything worse."

Her smile, beamed from her throne—far away and high above—was imperturbable.

"You *would* think that," she said.

Then, with a beneficent wave of her scepter, her eyes left mine, fixing instead upon the middle distance.

For other people were depending on her.

Grandchild

I gave birth to it, whatever it was: unspeakable monster.

"There," I said, and as I passed the bundle over to my mother, I dared her, with my burning eyes; I dared her to say it:

That the details mattered.

The Gingerbread Pox

A swirl of oven-warm crumbs composed the cloud, spicy and pungent. In their coordinated roiling, they took on the vague contours of a man.

"I'm the Gingerbread Pox!" the cloud announced, all abuzz, as it hovered before its latest target. "You can't avoid catching me!

"I've destroyed a Fairy Godmother, an Emperor who had no clothes, and an old woman and her seventeen children, all living in a shoe! And seven dwarfs, a peasant girl in a pumpkin coach, and a grandmother and her granddaughter, dressed in a red cloak! And three little pigs, three blind mice, an evil witch, and a Big Bad Wolf!

"And I'll destroy you too!"

Then, with one jittery, diaphanous limb, the Pox gestured behind it, to where, as far as the eye could reach, there were abandoned fields and silent villages. To the stacks and stacks, too, of unburied dead, all phlegmy lips and abscess-swollen skin.

But the fox—for whose benefit this speech had been delivered—simply leaned forward, feigning infirmity.

With a casual motion—whose meaning went unnoticed—he brushed a paw against his left forelimb where a tiny scar memorialized the puncture of a needle. And he remembered that childhood afternoon, long ago, when his sly, medically-savvy mother had prepared a protective potion from the pus of dead Pox victims—a magic called "vaccination."

"I can't quite hear you," the fox said, shaking his head. At the spicy smell of gingerbread, he secretly salivated; on the inside, too, his immune cells thrummed, waiting to assist with the digestion.

"Do come closer," he invited.

He Had Clearly Spent a Lot of Time Crafting an Appeal That Contained Exactly What I Wanted to Hear

"I don't want to hear it," I said.

The Greatest

In the ring, boxing gloves raised, Muhammad Ali invented sliced bread.

The slices were thin and precise, like the wings of a butterfly. And sweet and practical and wholesome, like the product of a bee.

"It ain't bragging if it's true," Ali said simply. And all around the ring, the crowd roared, brandishing the sandwiches they had prepared, slap slap, setting the meat easily within the pre-cut loaves that Ali had provided for them, no knives required.

F'ing the Ineffable

"How was it?" my friend asked. She flashed me a nasty smile, all lewdness and elbows, urging me to tell.

But I found, smiling back, that I really couldn't say.

The Girl Who Cried "Time Travel"

"I have come from ancient Rome!" I intended to say, returning from the supermarket, dressed in a tablecloth arranged like a toga, and brandishing a bundle of freshly purchased grapes.

But when I emerged from my car—my gag vehicle, my prop, which bristled with decorative dials...

Everything was silent.

All fragments and rubble.

"Look!" I began—for it reached me now, with a terrifying hollowness, that nothing remained *except* the script, nothing—to the tune of many centuries.

Eons.

"...from ancient Rome!" I finished to the dust; to the worn, empty earth; to the yellowed landscape; and to the vastly enlarged and worn-out sun.

But no one laughed.

Senility Breeds Contempt

"No," I said, reveling in the power differential. "*I* don't remember *you*."

Seven Choices

1. The Ruby Slippers

"Terminations aren't legal in Oz," Dorothy said. She touched her belly where the half-straw fetus twitched. On the sonographer's display, its half-sized brain floated, too small for its skull.

"That's why I came home."

2. Bibbity Bobbity Boo

"You are a whore," taunted the first stepsister.

"A filthy whore," added the second.

"Stay at home, or you will shame us," said the stepmother.

After their carriage rolled away, Cinderella curled up in the ashes, arms tight around her distended middle, regretting things.

But then, in a flash of light, her fairy godmother appeared. At the wand's touch, Cinderella's womb emptied, and her belly shrank, and she had a beautiful gown to wear, slim at the waist.

There was a coach, too, made of pumpkin. Footmen, who were actually mice. But Cinderella looked down, again and again, to admire her godmother's greatest miracle: her own lap, marvelously petite, as if nothing had ever happened.

"Dance with me," the prince entreated while her stepsisters howled with jealousy.

3. The Fairest of Them All

Snow White spoke in a furtive code: "Something to hurry my courses."

The peddler woman cackled knowingly at this and sold her a magic apple.

It went a bit wrong. Maybe the magic was too strong. Or maybe she swallowed too much. But her stomach burned, and her muscles seized up, and then she hit her head hard on the cobblestones.

When she woke, though, she was bleeding.

"It's gone," she assured Bashful when next they were alone.

4. A Midsummer's Morning

The donkey-headed creature left her bed. Months later, from her gut, Titania heard a small, tinny "Hee-Haw! Hee-Haw!" and a terrible fear seized her.

She summoned her attendants, Cobweb and Moth, and instructed them to fetch her a little eastern flower. It grew in a magic spot, where Athena's helm had once fallen to the earth, and women called it "evicting-unwanted-parasites."

Its petals were yellow, the color of regret.

5. The Seed of the Beast

The dates were wrong—too early. It had happened, almost surely, before the transformation, when her husband was still a monster.

Beauty would have learned to love a child like that. Furry, fanged, and horned. But she could not bear the possibility that it might grow to regret her decision, that it would withdraw from the world, as its father had, bitter in its deformity.

"Farewell," she wept, by way of apology.

6. A Baby Hare Is Called a "Leveret"

For her, the race was a pretext, a chance to visit the surgeon's cottage while evading her parents' curfew.

It took longer than she expected. Hours of forms and surgical prep, followed by hours of slow bleeding.

When she left the cottage, the sun was setting. Far in the distance, close to the finish line, she could just make out the outline of her competitor. One thick shell. Four thick legs.

"I've lost," she said, and began to laugh hysterically.

7. The First Little Pig

It was her fault, the forensics team informed her, for choosing straw. Clever girls used brick, and they were never assaulted.

"My fault?" she wondered. "My fault?" There was an

unbearable burden in that. And a wild rage. So later, after the team had gone, she covered her snout with her hooves and oinked until her throat was raw.

At a follow-up appointment, weeks later, they discovered a minute heartbeat, half-wolf. So she scheduled a procedure to end it. "Out," she whispered, with each scrape of the scalpel. "Out, out, out."

After her body was empty, though, the wolf stayed on in her head. "Your fault," he leered, over and over.

Ask an Evolutionary Biologist

She paused, mouth open. In her eyes you could see the temporal subtext smoldering: hundreds of millions of years.

What a stupid fucking question.

"Eggs came first," she said at last, clipped and politic. "Way, way before chickens."

The Velveteen Kitten

"Oh!" cried little Schrödinger, eight-year-old Erwin, of the creature, once composed of maroon plush that sat— real now, very real—at the bottom of his toy box.

"They *burned* you," he said wonderingly. "After my fever, they *burned* you."

"Yes," said the creature, purring enigmatically, "But."

Honestly

We argued—nastily—about parenting. And Santa Claus.

"So you just lie to your children routinely, then?" I said, as if summarizing. "For *years?*"

"That's not . . . " she objected.

"What is it like . . . " I said, leaning forward—still farther forward—and my voice went up, false, as if I were asking. "What is it like being such a liar?"

Frosty: A Man for All Seasons

Frosty the Gingerbread Man

"You can't catch me!" cried Frosty, nimble as a snowflake. "So many have tried!"

But the clever fox simply smiled, licked his lips, and flicked the "On" switch on his portable hairdryer.

Frosty the Trojan #1

There must have been some magic in that old arrow that he found. For when Frosty set it to his bow, it sped away, quick as thought, and penetrated the heel of the fleet-footed Achilles.

And the great warrior fell.

Frosty the Pillsbury Dough Man

"Hmm-hmm!" giggled Frosty, doubling over, as the children's mittened fingers sculpted the snow that would compose his stomach.

"Hmm-hmm!"

Frost Kent, aka Superman

His cape behind him was a ripple of red, topped by an "S" stitched in yellow buttons.

"I have only one vulnerability," he confessed to Lois as he lifted her mittened hand to the irregular semi-circle of pebbles that composed his lips.

"Heat."

Frostiet Tubman

She led them bravely, Thumpity, thump, thump; Thumpity, thump, thump, past dogs and bounty hunters, Thumpity, thump, thump; Thumpity, thump, thump, through hunger and heat, to the extreme north, where it was frozen year-round, and a snowman could be truly free.

Frosty the Strawman

"That's ludicrous!" cried the pundit. Then, with a deprecatory slap, she sent Frosty's magic hat tumbling.

Frosty fell silent. Then, under the lights of the debate hall, he began rapidly to ooze away—his argument nothing more than water.

Frosty, The Last Man on Earth

"I'm *still* not interested," she said coldly. And then she turned away into the lonely white, leaving the engagement button untouched in his wooden palm.

Frosty the Trojan #2

High in the tower, in a locked bedroom, Frosty kept his stolen bride. She was Troy's great prize, but also its bane, the curse that would eventually destroy the city and reduce its topless towers to water.

Helen, dear Helen, the warmest woman in the world.

Frostus, the Son of Man

A crown of thorns pierced His magic hat; the broomstick crucifix, too, on which He had been impaled was pitilessly stiff.

"Don't you cry," He told the children, managing a weak smile. He gestured to Heaven, where His Father lived and where His own body, once melted, would be transfigured to create spring rain.

"I'll be back again some day."

Frosty the Eggman

Frosty is the walrus, and his whiskers are broom bristles. And his eyes, like those of a dead dog, are made of coal.

See how he runs, like a pig from a gun, singing, "Catch me if you can."

Thumpity, thump thump; he's been a naughty boy.

Thumpity, thump thump; he's let his knickers down.

Mister city p'liceman sitting pretty hollers, "stop!"

But look at Frosty go, like Lucy in the sky. Don't you cry.

He's flying.

Frosty the Cave Man

For a thousand years, he had followed the receding glacier, hunting mammoths in its shadow. Until, after an atypically violent summer, what lay before him was only a roaring river, the glacier unreachable beyond it.

And Frosty's snow-sculpted brain, topped with its thick brow ridges, could conceive of no way forward.

So he sank down at last, the last of his people, and his broomstick spear rattled against bare rock.

Frosty the Boatman

For a fare of three buttons, he will wave you aboard.

He will not speak. And the only sounds will be the whispering scrape of his wooden arms as he sets himself to row and the rhythmic swish-swish of the River Styx sluicing through the bristles of his broomstick oars.

Frosty the Everyman

Because that's how it is, isn't it, for all of us? A brief, desperate struggle to run and to have some fun, and to do it *now*—Now, Now, Now—before we melt away.

Who Knew That Chess Involved So Much Strategy?

"I see like . . . like . . . two—no! no!—*god*, three things I can do!" I said at last, letting out a breath. And about me, the room, the atmosphere, shivered and popped, and all my neurons crackled.

"Four," she said.

Life, Not Baseball

One swing, a bad swing.

Strike one.

"Out," intoned the Reaper, grim in his umpire stripes.

Social Climber

Her detractors called her "conniving."

But her ambition—however one might characterize it—enabled her to marry well. Very well, and far above her station, to a breed of gentlemen and ladies who possessed no anuses.

"I wish to . . . take a solitary constitutional in the park," she said the morning of their marriage before hurrying alone into one of the tree-lined walks that crisscrossed the estate. And she lied like that; she lied and she lied and she lied again, every day, and, in furtive excursions down the shaded paths, she left the awful evidence of her low origins in one of a series of out-of-the-way places—pits of earth, which, however she might pretend, were not exactly gardens.

But the servants whispered.

And how long could one hide?

"Darling . . . " said her husband to her at last with a look that was more than wounded—betrayed. And something else—revulsion—set upon those perfect lips that proceeded, inside, to a tube that descended, genteelly, no farther than his throat.

"My love . . . " she began. "Reverend lord!" she corrected as his expression become harder. "I . . . " but there were no plausible denials to make—not anymore—nothing she could say. And the rest, after that, was a useless slur—fetid syllables emitted with weak swallows from her own throat, which extended darkly down and down and down.

As if he might forgive her.

If You Had Any Idea What I Was Referring To, You Would Be Laughing Really Hard Right Now

But.

Lights, Camera...

In the 1970s, the light reached us at last.

Light from long, long ago.

And sourced from a galaxy far, far away.

Eye hovering, close to the lens, he let out a breath—this young director, fresh from the set of *American Graffiti*.

And swallowed.

"Start filming," he said in a hiss to his crew of telescope flunkies and astronomy teamsters. "*Start filming*."

When Frankly Met Surely

Do you come here often? asked Surely.

Periodically, said Frankly.

How do you propose to impress me?

Coyly.

Affectedly.

Bombastically.

Hilariously.

Would you like to . . . make love? asked Frankly.

Urgently, thought Surely.

But instead—chastely—she whispered: Eventually.

So they married—

Prematurely. Ill-advisedly. Hurriedly.

Forever and ever? asked the officiant.

(Presumably, thought Frankly.)

(Plausibly, thought Surely.)

Indubitably, they answered.

And commenced to live . . .

Cheaply, said Surely.

Extravagantly, countered Frankly.

And: Argumentatively.

Stop calling me "Shirley," said Surely.

Said Frankly: My dear, I don't give a damn.

But reconciled:

... vigorously ...

... ecstatically ...

... carelessly ...

Are you ... pregnant? asked Frankly.

Hardly, scoffed Surely.

Conceivably, admitted Surely.

Doubly, announced the sonographer.

Oh, said Frankly—shell-shockedly.

No, said Surely—delusionally.

Endurably ...? asked Frankly.

Interminably, said Surely, heavily.

Miserably, said Surely, crowning.

Preventably, sighed Frankly and scheduled a vasectomy.

And the months passed ...

... noisily ...

... groggily ...

. . . ickily . . .

But occasionally: adorably.

And sporadically: rewardingly.

And the decades, too, slipped away from them.

Swimmingly; drearily.

Excruciatingly; equivocally.

Durably; poignantly.

Perfectly.

Then: creakingly, dementedly, arthritically.

And on that final morning, amid the sheets, gnarled hands entwined about their withered hips: exquisitely.

How did they go? asked their septuagenarian twins.

Simultaneously, said the coroner.

Rebecca Opens up a Can!
and There's Dinner!

"You know," I cackled to my daughter-in-law with a twitch of my nose, "I only say these things to be hateful."

"That is precisely the reason I married your son, Agnes," she said, and her nose twitched back.

"Bitch," I said archly.

But my eyes sparkled. And my voice trembled—

How perfect she was.

They Shared Custody

It was one of those car accidents, a really really bad one, one that split space and time.

In one version of the accident, my Dad died. In an adjacent reality, my Mom died.

I died, too, in one or the other.

But that distinction mattered less.

Because, though adults could not cross the shatter lines dividing two divergent scatterings of the same event, children could.

One day, when I came of age, I would have to choose.

But until then, I spent the first and third weeks of the month with my Mom and the second and fourth weeks of the month with my Dad.

And—for it seemed only fitting—I brought flowers.

"Mom," I said as we stood together over Dad's grave, "do you like gardenias?"

"Dad," I said as we stood together over Mom's grave, "do you like roses?"

I'm Not a Bad Person on the Outside, Just Deep Down

"So . . . friends?" he said with a passable smile.

A (Condensed) Dictionary of Mythological Characters

Adonis-Argus

He was a beautiful youth, possessed of one hundred eyes. But he scorned women, preferring cows.

Oedipus-Orpheus

He consigned his mother to hell. But then he looked back as he exited the pit and perceived that he desired her.

Pandora-Phaeton

From the box, while her father slept, she released the sun, which burned all the world.

Priapus-Procrustes

To humanity, he gave the gift of penis standardization. He cut penises that were too long and stretched penises that were too short. After that, all men were the same.

Saturn-The Sirens

To his sons, he sang haunting lullabies. Then he devoured them.

Just Us

We had a book group, an exclusive one, and this would be our first meeting.

No men—obviously.

Rule #1.

And no people of color. Though not, of course, from any intention. Quite the contrary.

That was exactly the sort of demographic difficulty we would be talking about.

Exactly.

And no one without a college degree.

"Well!" I said, lifting our first text as my eyes stung: the possibility. "Let's talk about human diversity!"

And we turned the page.

Perhaps I Cannot Hold a Candle to You, But I Can Set You on Fire

Whoosh.

Are You?

"Everyone will hurt you," she said.

"But are you worth it?" I asked bitterly while chewing my lower lip for nerves. "Worth hurting for?"

Her eyes skittered away. And from her own sleeve, tentatively (a question), she removed a hand that was even more disfigured than mine, bruised and welted with a range of marks: old scabs and new, and a stump in the fourth position, no finger.

"I don't know," she said.

Sasquatch Rapunzel

Hair, hair.

And more hair.

"What were you expecting?" she asked the Prince.

½ mv²

We met in physics class fall semester.

During the term, we studied together in the library: mass, velocity, and acceleration; variables and equations.

Energy.

Then, for six weeks after exams were over, we went sledding almost every day. We tried every hill there was, everything close to campus, but we especially favored the biggest ones, which were grandiosely—but also, not so grandiosely—named "Falcon's Peak" and "Dead Man's Ridge."

They were very tall.

Up to the top, part hiking, part running, and our legs ached—all that potential energy accumulated, P.E. = mgh, where m was our mass, g the gravity, and h the height—once we were there, suspended at the edge, the white and the crunch of it, extending like a promise, glittery and steep.

Possibility—and we felt it together, sitting there, each in our own sled, side by side. A quick look at one another, then below. That taste of it—possibility becoming, as we tipped, as we *tipped* . . .

Inevitability.

Slow at first.

Then faster.

Down those hills with him, over and over, two sleds in coordinated trajectories, screaming through crystals, powder, ice.

Friends.

Weeks like that, with warm drinks afterwards, warming together, first in little shops along University Avenue; then, increasingly, when the buildings opened again, with the re-initiation of the term, spring semester, in the cafe at the Student Union.

Friends—building to good, building to better, and as we built, we spoke in a curious and evolving dialect that was rooted in physics, where it began, but now it was more than that. In it, I told him things, more and more, things I had never told anyone else.

And stuff, too. I told him stuff. So much *stuff*.

Almost everything.

Until one morning in the Student Union, on a couch beside the fire, so early on a Saturday, the whole room atypically empty; just us. Hot chocolate in my hands and my face raw with cold, still painfully warming, this laughter about light things.

It was like being drunk.

And my heart beat, crazy, crazy, more than equations, and sensing wildly—or merely wishfully—a moment, I croaked it out, all in a rush, my voice gone fuzzy, together with my chest. Everything, *everything*, all in one word:

"Kinetic?" I asked.

Silence, sudden silence.

Eyes. I couldn't stop looking at him, even as I understood I had ruined all of it—this thing I built with him; the friendship we made, over all those weeks, bit by bit and little step, gravity, height, mass, and now with this "Kinetic?" question and confession, I had thrown it all away, down and down and down, and I was crashing with it, stupid, stupid, stupid.

What had I done?

Just *eyes*, strange eyes, but he wasn't saying anything, and . . .

What had I done?

"Kinetic," he said at last. His voice, too, was strange and scratchy. And his silence—and I understood this now, I understood it, with a small, revelatory shiver—had been the time it takes for a person to swallow, for a throat to clear.

And my heart . . .

Eyes. Hands. Cold-chapped lips. Close, now so *close*. Possibility, tipping into . . .

Inevitability.

Slow at first.

Then faster.

Are Bears Catholic?

He emerged, at last, from the woods.

"What were you doing, Your Holiness?" asked the cleric.

Multitasking

I had it. I would score political points with the group by affecting an outward show of alignment with her. But I would insult her, too, unmistakably—but irreproachably and in full view—under the cover of a compliment.

Two birds, one email.

And the air about me hummed, taut with the passivity of my aggression.

Perfect push, yes. Perfect now.

Send.

The Abdication

He was the Prince of Heaven.

But he gave that up for their mother at—yes!—the moment he saw her: lovely, mortal Elena, in her simple white dress beside the temple.

Their children heard the story many, many times, how, for their mother, he descended into the filthy welter of this lower world: tuberculosis, dysentery, and typhus. How, over his Family's objections, he sacrificed everything: his place in the Succession, the immortalizing apples from the Garden of Dawn, his seat in the Chariot of the Sun.

For love.

"Daddy," said their second daughter as she died, wistful and feverish, four years old. "I wish I had been born a Princess."

In My Calendar

"Hey, 1999 self!" I cried. "Let's have lunch!"

So we did. In the same spot as always, third table from the back.

But she looked right through me.

You Can Clean Out the Litter Box, Once In a While

I didn't even want cats.

But I *did* it, for him. I burned through a series of reproductive interventions: implantation of the feline donor's embryos in my human womb and all the painful and humiliating rest of it. And hours of false labor, too—bruised and clawed and irreparably distended—prior to an emergency Caesarean.

"*So*," I said to him through slitted teeth. "So, so, so . . .

The Agnostic Gospels:
Variations on a Theme

Of the non-traditional gospels, the most notorious are the Gnostic Gospels, which were unearthed in Egypt in 1945 after a 1,500-year burial.

But here—less known and unearthed elsewhere—are a few others.

The Epiblastic Gospel

Animated by the Holy Spirit, He burrowed into the Virgin's womb and grew and grew and grew.

And when He acquired the general shape of a vertebrate embryo—at that curious stage where there exists very little external difference between a sheep and a man—His translucent lips vibrated in the amniotic fluid in order to form these words:

"I am the Lamb of God."

The Sarcastic Gospel

"Born of a Virgin . . . ," said the Oriental king, rolling his eyes. He had traveled a long way, perhaps, and all at the promise of a star, but he was not an utter fool.

"Riiighhht . . . ," he said in an exaggerated stage whisper, while congenially elbowing Joseph.

The Caustic Gospel

It was a tricky chemistry—water into wine. And—son of God, or not—it was nothing that a child ought to have undertaken.

He would retain, long after, the shattering guilt of it—a shadow, which persisted over the whole of His ministry.

Water, transformed, not into wine, but instead into acid.

At the toast at Cana, the liquid sloshed, hissing, over the brim. And, when the bride and groom—and the entire wedding party—raised their cups, their throats were horribly burned and their faces permanently disfigured.

"My God," He would wonder that night and every night as He grew into a man, "Why did you abandon Me?"

The Diabetic Gospel

The hypodermic needle was a miracle in its own right— sleek and sharp, and with intricate retractable parts.

But more striking still was the liquid it delivered.

Under its influence, dying men lost their gauntness and became rosy-cheeked and whole.

"I cure you in the name of insulin," said Jesus solemnly, each time He depressed the plunger.

The Apoplectic Gospel

Year after year, the fig tree had been barren.

So Jesus punched it and He punched it until the flesh of His knuckles peeled back.

"Ligneous trash!" He yelled as He ripped off the branches, one by one, and then smashed the entire trunk to sawdust. "Selfish heap of twigs!"

The Hypnotic Gospel

"You are feeling very alive," Jesus said to Lazarus. And He set the watch chain to sway, rhythmically and persuasively, before the dead man's closed lids.

The Autistic Gospel

His intonation was flat. His gestures were awkward. And He stood too close.

"No, thank you," said the leper firmly, too disconcerted by His affect to really listen to the offer.

"Really . . . ," murmured the fishermen uneasily, until finally, finding no polite pretext for escape, they simply slipped away, mid-parable, stifling uncomfortable laughter.

So He spoke to the wind, instead, and to the birds He promised grace.

The Homoerotic Gospel

He washed my feet, attentive and slow. His fingers against my instep were terrifyingly—and exquisitely—warm.

"What is it, Peter?" He asked when I made a small, involuntary sound. His eyes, meeting mine, were wide and dark and beautiful.

"The tension," I said, though through my constricted throat, it came out as barely a whisper.

The Slapstick Gospel

"I said, lepers, you knuckleheads!" Jesus shouted, gesturing angrily toward the pack of unruly—and entirely unwanted—leopards, which were now making mischief in the marketplace.

Then, with a growl, He grabbed Thomas by a tuft of his curly hair and pulled back hard.

"Ow! Ow! Ow!" Thomas cried, snatching at his scalp and dancing for pain.

Jesus came after Peter, too, two fingers extended. But Peter set his palm flat and with it extended the bridge of his nose, so that even as Jesus jabbed, his eyes remained safe.

"Nyuk! Nyuk!" cried Peter.

The Arctic Gospel

Across the ice floes, the crowds hurried, eager to taste of the loaves and the fishes.

And enjoy it they did, devouring every fish to the last, though they mostly left behind the bread.

To His sermon, however, they were largely indifferent. So, eventually, crying, "Arkh! Arkh! Arkh!" they lurched away disinterestedly at the propulsion of their flippers and retreated back into the sea.

The Transatlantic Gospel

After a four-month journey, the Captain and His apostles disembarked, wobbly-legged, from their tiny fishing vessel.

"We come bearing the Word of my Father," He said, smiling disarmingly at the natives who met Him at the shore. "And smallpox."

Then He showed them the pustules on His hands where the disease had spread, and He urged them to probe the marks with their own fingers, so they would believe.

The Lactic Gospel

He squeezed His nipples carefully, filling each of the twelve cups equitably, up to the brim. The liquid was warm and sweet, sweeter than the milk of any cow.

When the cups were full and the pressure relieved, He tucked His breasts back into His nursing bra.

"Take," He instructed the apostles, handing each of them a cup. "And drink of Me."

The Socratic Gospel

"Therefore," said Jesus, "money-changers are fish and Samaritans are grasshoppers."

The disciples stared at Him, glassy-eyed.

Something had gone wrong, somewhere. And once again, starting from perfectly sensible precepts, He had led them, piecewise and via apparently impeccable logic, to a conclusion that was utterly silly.

This had been going on for days.

Judas snorted, breaking the uncomfortable silence.

"Drink this, my Lord," he said. And then, with an exaggerated motion—not in the least bothering to hide it—he emptied a vial of hemlock into Jesus's wine.

The Athletic Gospel

During the entire first day and a half of the decathlon, He shouldered the Cross.

Crippled by the burden of it, He lurched slowly: last in the 100-meter dash, last in the 400-meter dash, and last in the 110-meter hurdles.

And oh, how the crowds jeered.

But on the afternoon of the second day, as He prepped for the pole vault, something shifted.

Down the field He pounded, faster than He—or anyone—ever had. Then, with a deft motion, He planted the upper tip of the Cross on the runway, just before the mat, and went soaring into the sky.

The bar, far beneath Him, did not even quiver.

The Robotic Gospel

With the addition of each new nail, wires crunched and circuits frizzled.

"Bee-oop! Bee-oop!" He cried mournfully. His eyes flashed madly—0101010101. Arcs of current, too, extended from His chest, static and blue: Blatt! Blatt! Blatt!; each arc weaker than the one that preceded it.

Until, with a final twitch, He went quite still.

But then, furtively, from beneath her cloak, Mary Magdalene removed a package of fresh batteries.

The Intergalactic Gospel

On the second day, unable to wait, Peter rolled away the stone.

"I will take You to Your Father," he promised in a whisper while cradling the limp, cold head.

Mary Magdalene beamed them aboard the ship. Thomas, the medic, enclosed the Body in a stasis chamber. The chamber would forestall any further decomposition, ensuring that, when they did reach His Father—however long that would take—a true Resurrection would still be possible.

Peter settled into the Captain's chair. From there, he stared out, grim and determined, into the vast expanse that lay before them, where no man—but only God—had ever been before.

"Maximum warp," he instructed Mary Magdalene.

The ship shuddered. Then, through the viewing screen, all of the stars blurred together into a single smear, and they proceeded into Light.

Lonely

With a regimen of Nix, I rid myself of the lice. And with two doses of pyrantel pamoate, I eradicated my pinworms.

All gone.

"How do you feel?" she asked me afterwards, the Saturday counter pharmacist who was the closest creature I might any longer call a friend.

"Well," I said, trying bravely to smile. "I—"

On the Edge

There was an eternal character to it. Which was not hell, exactly—

No.

But . . .

"You're still not quite on it," she whispered.

"Now?" he asked hopefully.

"No," she said.

Two Roads Converged In a Wood

I recognized her immediately, even at the shock of it: the alternative version of myself that studied abroad in Germany for a semester rather than staying home.

"Wie geht's?" I asked her, thick-tongued.

Jealous.

"Fine," she laughed. Her German, in the end, and this came out quickly, was no better than mine, and she showed me the tattoo she'd gotten there, which was eerily—impossibly—similar to the one I'd gotten at the local parlor.

Down the path, framed by trees, we continued in quiet conversation, talking of choices and personal significance, each of us, at intervals, catching the other's eye: synchronized, increasingly, in essentially every way, but also in *this*—which hurt, in a way, more than my jealousy had—

That it had made absolutely no difference.

My Breasts Are Up Here

Eight months pregnant.

"Hey, buddy!" I shouted.

I Met Heathcliff on the Moors

I was forever meeting Heathcliff on the moors.

I presented him with a gift: fish on a platter, dark and dead. And he gave me a jagged, brooding look, straight from *Wuthering Heights*.

"Cat," I said, "why can't I stop loving you?"

Life Purpose

"You know," he said, "you need to stop at some point."

"I don't," I returned. And I continued, stroke, stroke, to excavate the remaining peanut butter from the jar, which was never quite empty.

Never.

For the War Effort

It was a civil war of the most bloody, brutal sort, not East vs. West, or brother vs. brother.

But rather: Past vs. Future.

They (the Future) had a staggering technological advantage. Our skies were filled with weapons that we did not understand, our cities pillaged and brutalized by invasions for which we could devise no shields.

But our position gave us another kind of advantage.

Just one, really.

So, since there was no other choice—none at all—we exploited it.

To our hands—violently, unnaturally—we transferred bundles of our own flesh, uprootings of potentialities that many of us at one time had wanted very much.

(That I, too, had wanted so very, very much.)

So it felt like more than war, this sacrifice.

But we were members of the Great Generation. The Final Generation.

We could not let them win.

Around the fires we gathered, in our public squares:

heat and whoosh and flicker, in long long lines, extending through cities and countryside, and we roared as the smoke ascended, for we could see it— Yes! Yes! Yes!—the count of our enemies/descendants, diminishing across distance; the shrinking phalanxes of their armies in the sky; the dots of their ground troops viewed through our spyglasses, fewer and fewer; and we, yes, we, determined and resourceful we (and here the roar went up again!), reducing the numbers of this superior force at this clever remove, as we could not in direct combat.

Into heat, into plumes of smoke, into Never-Was.

Attrition and annihilation.

To the front of the line—my turn—I pushed at last, with thousands still behind me, thousands upon thousands, each with our bundles of flesh: compatriots-in-war, each of us hunching for pain, hobbled by the recency of our surgical scars.

"'U' is for victory!" I intoned fiercely.

And I cast my Uterus onto the fire.

An Awkward Conversation That Neither of Us Can Seem to Get Out Of

We were deep, too deep, before either of us realized.

"Help!" she screamed.

"Help," I whispered.

But we only had each other.

In the Old Country, There Is Only One Restaurant, and on the Menu, There Is Only One Thing

She spat out the words, and with a sweeping gesture, she incorporated the entirety of the shopping mall food court into her disdain.

Then, in a nostalgic tone—mouth puckering beneath her shawl—she continued: "And they are out of it."

Simple Tastes

"Do you think," I said as my voice contracted and my heart beat fast, "you could . . . just lean over me, just loom over me, and . . . and . . . grunt?"

"Grruh?" he said uncertainly.

But I nodded, blood in my ears like thunder.

So he stepped closer.

Simple Tastes, Part 2:
Then He Grew a Beard

And . . .

Imaginary Friend

Flowers and teacups, cupcakes and lace.

Everything perfect.

"I don't like you," she shouted at me from the doorway, over the heads of the other guests—a velour rabbit in a frock coat and a bear in a satin ball gown. "I've never ever ever ever *ever* liked you."

"Okay!" I agreed, hopping up from the Playskool table settings in order to call solicitously after her. "So . . . see you tomorrow?"

This Story, I Promise You, Is Going to Have a Punchline

But no setup.

Four Christmas Miracles

1

Three wise men, copulating in the straw, father a thrice-wise child. They dress him in gold, anoint him with myrrh, then remodel his forehead, using scraps borrowed from Frankenstein's monster. Later, taking the name of Ramses, the boy will single-handedly construct the City of Rome, while passionately declaring, *"Liberté, égalité, fraternité!"*

2

A snowman, brought to life by action of magic top hat, passes unharmed through the Magic Fire. Then he claims his Valkyrie bride, who sleeps on the top of the mountain. In consummating their union, he begets twins upon her: one, an extraordinary deaf-blind girl, whom an astonished world will ever afterwards remember as Helen Keller; the other, a philanthropic boy, favoring self-expression through fruit, who will take the name Johnny Appleseed.

3

A wealthy miser is visited by a series of ghosts. The first, the scarecrow, forces him to revisit his agrarian childhood and the trauma of the Irish potato famine. The second, the tinman, confronts him with the evils of the Industrial Revolution, which occupy his present. The third, the lion, warns him of a disturbing future, in which genetic manipulation has so blurred the distinctions between humanity and other life that men assimilate their nutrients via root-like limbs extended into the soil, and animals can talk.

4

A woman cuts her hair in order to purchase a watch chain. Her lover sells his watch to purchase a set of hair combs. "How tragic!" they cry. Then, with a coordinated heave, they cast their useless gifts into the embers. The action produces a massive fireball, which whooshes up the chimney. In the blaze of it, the Big Bad Wolf is incinerated, together with the One Ring of Sauron, and Odysseus's Trojan horse. A contingent of Greek soldiers, badly burned, tumble onto the grate, their ambitions halted, and King Priam, emerging from the cinders, announces that *now*, now that the course of Western Civilization has been altered, Old Yeller—his vulnerable heel so recently (and triply) punctured by (a) Robin Hood's arrow, (b) the ensorcelled tip of an enchanted spinning wheel, and (c) the Chicxulub meteorite, whose impact precipitated a mass extinction at the end of the Mesozoic—will, like Tiny Tim, recover from his rabies. Old Yeller, like Tiny Tim, will walk.

Old Yeller barks triumphantly. And while bells tinkle madly, everywhere—rung by Quasimodo and the Phantom of the Opera, both grinning madly—and while Eli Whitney—in complementary time, beats upon his cotton gin—a chorus of sugarplum fairies—giggling cherubically, adorably, within the silvery tangle of King Priam's beard—add this to the chorus:

"It's a wonderful life. It is. It is.

"It's a wonderful, wonderful life."

Double-Decker Bus

I spent most of my life in America.

After my move to London, my instinct, whenever I crossed the street, was to look left first, then right.

But with conscious—and constant—drilling, I corrected myself:

right first,

then left.

Until eventually, there came a point—a momentous, transitional instant—where the two states were superimposed: left AND right, one instinct layered over the other, one inclination perfectly balanced by its opposite; and I looked only straight ahead.

Just once.

I Have Never Been Published by the *Paris Review*, but I Have Engineered a Surefire Method for Doing So; It Involves a Spreadsheet

"After all," continued Lucia, "I am a graduate of Alloisius."

None of us had ever heard of the Alloisius Writing Workshop in any context outside of Lucia. But still—we heard about it a lot.

That's how we knew it was prestigious.

"It's about finding correlations," said Lucia, shrewdly, as she distributed a stack of recent issues to each member of our writing group.

"First," she said crisply, opening a fresh Excel file, "we count the number of e's."

Alternative Histories

A Thousand Ships

"Call it 'Helen,'" the swan instructed her when it had finished, leaving her sticky and bruised.

Then it flew away.

"Never," she thought.

After the abortion, she traveled often, dodging the god's thunderbolts. It was hard, all the journeying, because the water triggered her nightmares, and she felt the weight of feathers pushing her down whenever the boat rocked.

But she survived.

When she was very old, she visited Troy. She craned her neck, the better to admire its fabled towers.

That action, too, was briefly triggering since it reminded her of Mt. Olympus and therefore of the god. (And yet, didn't a good many things hurt—even beautiful things—after that hour at the lake?)

But she smiled wanly at it anyway, at the spectacle of that fortified city—as bright and invulnerable as she had once been.

Beowulf's Trophy

That year, when the fish died, she starved, and the little gob inside her did too. Or it should have done. But it continued to grow, a lump against her ribs.

"There is nothing to eat, Grendel," she told it. "You must go away."

But it didn't. So she crawled out of the lake, one damp evening, and visited the herbalist who lived on the shore. Then she cut off her claws—for that was all she had—and bartered them in exchange for two pills.

Years later—once Hrothgar's ancestors had established settlements—she discovered a surer source of food. On nights when the rain was heavy, enough to keep her gill flaps moist, she crept into the newcomers' halls and selected a meaty specimen.

She kept her abductions infrequent. And she left no bloody trail. In her care, she usually left it plausible that her victims had simply wandered away of their own volition, lost in the Danish mists.

Let Down Your Hair

When she was pregnant, she craved salad. So she climbed over the witch's wall one moonless evening, hoping to collect a few leaves.

She should have passed unseen. But the witch caught her and threatened to kill her, and forced her to sign a cruel contract.

According to the terms, the woman's child would rot away its entire life inside an isolated prison. The witch's potions, too, would render the child monstrously hirsute, so that its neck and spine would twist, damaged by the weight.

A month later, once she'd had time to reconsider—and to grieve—the woman delivered a dirty bundle to the witch. It contained a minute, motionless creature, many weeks too young.

"Here is Rapunzel," she said.

So She Whipped Them All Soundly and Sent Them to Bed

There was a young woman who lived in a shoe. The shoe was her own design project, and with it, she earned a master's degree in sartorial architecture.

She had never wanted a family. So after that first—and terrifying—contraceptive failure, she had an abortion. Then, months later, after a second scare, she scheduled a hysterectomy.

Afterwards, in dizzying succession, she landed seven contracts, each more lucrative than the one before:

1) a village made of buttons

2) a ballroom made of tuxedos and pearl necklaces

3) a series of municipal pools made of recycled swimwear

4) an apartment complex for bachelor gentlemen, built from cravats and top hats

5) a sports arena made of scrimmage jerseys

6) a hospital made of linen sheets, surgical gowns, and autoclaved bandages

7) a French hotel made of lingerie

After her rise, the woman lunched at the best restaurants—seasonal soups, paired with artisanal breads, slice after exquisitely-crafted slice. Then, if Rome called, or New York or Tokyo or Paris, as they often did, speaking with excited agitation about some daunting new project—*Could she do it? Could she?*—she responded airily and between mouthfuls:

"I know exactly what to do."

When Nietzsche Met Quantum Physics Met Galileo

The abyss stares. But the position of its eyes are undecided, indeterminately quivering, until you stare—stare back.

And yet it moves.

Spit or Swallow?

Pride.

In my mouth, a burning conviction of my own preeminence, so caustic and so bitter that my cheeks began to pucker. Then scar.

But I couldn't bear to do either.

Retribution

"Grandfather..." I began when he appeared in my time and at my doorstep—a specter out of paradox.

"Yes?" he said with a terrible smile.

"*How—?*"

"Why do you think?" he returned, electing to address a different question.

And he lifted his pistol.

Fleeting

They came to me, these mortals, to my very doorstep: scholar-priests and poet-kings, having ascended, somehow, all the steps of Heaven, in order to visit me.

And to philosophize.

"But even if *life* is short," asserted one, "*art* is long."

"Oh?" I said.

Piqued.

So, with a thought, I burned their great library at Alexandria, sent a great flood to dash their paintings and sculptures into fragments, and cast the remnants to the bottom of the sea.

Then, with another, I permitted their world to age into darkness, then light: pigments, parchments, and memorials, devoured by their dying sun.

All in a blink.

"Who was that?" asked my consort sleepily from the other room.

"Someone," I said uncertainly, trying to remember.

Imprecision

"But, Mother," she said softly, above the piles of gifts and the heap of discarded wrapping paper, "I don't *want* any of these things."

"I know," I said with a manic sadness, my heart welling. "That's why I had to get you more."

Different Boxes

On their third date, Pandora began to open up.

In her childhood, she said, there had been . . . things.
Harrowing specters (and here she wept) that emerged
from the basement: malevolent figures—all the Sorrows
of the World—that burned her again, in memory,
whenever she touched them.

Her eyes, like scars.

"Well," said Schrödinger—two uncomfortable coughs.
"I had a cat."

Are These the Shadows of the Things That Will Be? Or the Shadows of the Things That May Be Only?

It was a night of bells. And visions. And, when she woke, she tied her dressing gown hastily and rushed onto the balcony.

"You there, boy," she cried."What day is it?"

"Why, it's Christmas day!" he answered.

Oh, she swallowed.

Still time.

"Run down to the corner market," she said with a delighted laugh, "and buy me a package of prophylactics! The biggest you can find!"

And she threw him down a twenty pound note—then a second—which drifted down, beautifully down, into the new snow.

What It's All About

·The Hokey Pokey.

·The #42.

·But the Greatest of these is Love.

About the Author

Rachel Rodman writes many forms of experimental fiction, both short and long. She is the author of a collection of literary recipes and a series of quantum cloud narratives featuring Erwin Schrödinger. Her Ph.D. is in biochemistry. In the classroom, she is developing ways to teach genetics and chemistry through creative writing and evolution through art.

—www.rachelrodman.com

Shanti Arts

Nature • Art • Spirit

Please visit us online
to browse our entire book catalog,
including poetry collections and fiction,
books on travel, nature, healing, art,
photography, and more.

Also take a look at our highly
regarded art and literary journal,
Still Point Arts Quarterly, which
may be downloaded for free.

www.shantiarts.com